T0368416

IT LINGERS IN MY DREAMS

Laura L. Bates

WestBow Press books may be ordered through booksellers or by contacting:

WestBow Press
A Division of Thomas Nelson & Zondervan
1663 Liberty Drive
Bloomington, IN 47403
www.westbowpress.com
844-714-3454

Interior Image Credit: Laura L. Bates

ISBN: 979-8-3850-3498-7 (sc)
ISBN: 979-8-3850-3499-4 (e)

Library of Congress Control Number: 2024920639

Print information available on the last page.

WestBow Press rev. date: 09/27/2024

It Lingers in My Dreams is dedicated to those I met and worked with on my second short-term missionary trip to Uganda. They were my inspiration and mentors. I appreciate the work they do year after year, spreading the gospel to Uganda. Their names have been changed out of respect. I also thank my husband Paul for his support and editing help, as well as Taylor, Adelaide, and Lisa for their input and encouragement.

CONTENTS

CHAPTER ONE

People say that once you get Uganda in your blood, it's hard to get it back out. The warm and humid air caught Anne up short as she stepped out of the airport in Entebbe. She had been homesick for three years for this foreign land. She stood still a moment, taking it all in.

Flies buzzed lazily as she set her bags down to wait. A grey cheeked mangabey monkey sat, as though waiting as well, a short distance away. People streamed out of the small airport-most were black skinned, the women with colorful skirts and headwraps, chattering away in an unknown language. One man heaved first a large box, and then other luggage onto the top of a van. He took a long time tying everything down. Anne watched a group of children who ran excitedly about, the boys without shirts, dodging in and out among other travelers and chasing the monkey away. They finally bounded into the van at the order of an older woman, and with the children hanging out of the windows, the van started slowly off, bumping away down the rutted road. The monkey returned to sit.

The smell of red dust met Anne's nostrils, and her face began to sweat. Carefully she sat on the sturdiest part of her suitcase, feet together, and swatted at a tsetse fly that tried to settle on her bare ankle. She felt the thin blouse she wore begin to stick to her skin. She watched people leave – lovers, children, friends, and the parking area emptied. An official in a brown uniform who had stood at the exit disappeared behind the glass door. Then, just as she began to feel conspicuous and alone, another car pulled in and she recognized the smiling face of Devon the driver. She rose as he sprang from the small car, unfolding his long legs - greeting her exuberantly.

"Miss Anne," he said in slightly broken English. "You are most welcome."

After fitting her luggage, one piece in the trunk and one on the back seat, he settled her next to himself. The trip to the missionary complex was a bumpy one and Anne leaned back against the cracked leather seat. Fields of sorghum passed by and she saw African Flame trees with their red blossoms. The window was partially open and flowering plants along the road let off a scent mingled with the dust – a scent that couldn't be identified, but brought back with directness her previous short trip to Uganda almost two years ago. It was an achingly sweet memory.

About 45 minutes later they entered Kampala, passing through honking traffic and dust. Chaotic markets congested both sides of the road and Devon drove skillfully through intersections, just missing the bicycles and pedestrians, swerving quickly around buses and other vehicles. To Anne it was exciting. She had no notion of being involved in the too frequent traffic accidents – after which drivers would stand yelling endlessly at each other regarding who was at fault. At long last, they were in the outskirts of the city, and the congestion thinned. Eventually, after multiple turns, they pulled up to a tall wall broken by a gate. Devon leapt out and swung the right side open, then regaining his seat, drove them into the mission's compound.

The compound itself was an oasis of beauty, with an acre

of lush lawn, avocado trees and carefully cultivated hibiscus and rose bushes. It had the air of a private sanctuary – shielded from Kampala's noise and frenzy by its tall walls. Through the greenery Anne spied the big house – a large white structure that housed missionary Bess and her "adopted daughters." Another, smaller house sat attached to the side and this housed missionary Elaine. As Anne stepped out of the car, she saw Missionary Bess exiting the big house, making her way towards her. In a few moments, she was embraced by Bess's strong arms, and pulled into her ample bosom. Bess was a stout white woman with long black hair beginning to grey, which was pulled up in a bun on her head. Her attitude, as Anne recalled, was kindly but no nonsense, as she had a complex to run, and students to look after. A certain shy gratitude crept over Anne as she recounted her flight out, and the layover in Amsterdam. It would be her first time to join a real "missionary team," as a fellow worker rather than a guest. As of yet, she wasn't quite sure what that might entail, except that she would be leading bible studies and working with the local population.

"You remember my daughter Joy" Bess commented, as a beautiful young woman joined them. Joy's teeth gleamed in her dark face as she bent her knees slightly and murmured "mum," grasping Anne's hands in her own warm ones.

"Oh yes," breathed Anne. "How wonderful to see you again, Joy."

"Things haven't changed a lot since you were here last," said Bess, "except that we added on another wing to the school. Let's walk over to your quarters and leave you to rest a while. We'll look at the school later. It has been a long journey over for you."

Anne nodded gratefully. Anne's small apartment, she found, was across the property next to the church.

As they left her there, Bess added, "dinner at the big house at six o'clock."

Anne opened and ducked through the narrow doorway into what would be her new home for the next few years, if all went well. It consisted of a small kitchen, a slightly larger living area with a comfortable looking chair, a bedroom with a twin-size bed with its requisite mosquito netting, and a bathroom. A bathroom was separated from the bedroom by a beaded doorway. It contained a toilet, sink, and shower without a curtain. A bucket of water sat on the floor to flush the toilet with. Everything had a slightly musty odor, as though the space hadn't been used for some time, though it had obviously been outfitted for her. In the kitchen she found silverware, cups, and other necessities. There was a small bookcase in the living space where she saw a handful of old books, one of which was on the life of Hudson Taylor. His famous quote came to mind – "God's work done in God's way will never lack God's supplies."

After the two-bedroom apartment she had occupied back in the states, the accommodations were modest in the extreme. But then she couldn't expect to be housed somewhere like the big house. Anne sank into the cushioned chair and took stock of the situation. She had done it. Against the advice of several people, and with encouragement of others, she had actually flown half-way around the world by herself to be a missionary! She was truly giving herself over to God's will for her life and sacrificing for Him. She felt a sense of satisfaction, as well as a slightly hollow feeling in the pit of her stomach.

Several hours later Anne entered the Big House by a stone pathway that wound behind a retaining wall and then through a covered porch area and arched entryway. It was as it sounded – a big white-washed house with red brick flooring. She removed her shoes on the patio, and stepped around a large dog that lay there. It was unfamiliar to her. It lifted its head briefly, but seemed unconvinced about moving its position. Anne patted its head, and Joy, greeting her at the doorway, said, "His name is Sampson."

"I hope I'm not too late."

"Not at all," said Bess, waving her in. "Join the gang."

Seated at the big wooden table were Devon, Elaine, two unknown young women, a young child not more than two, and another older man that Anne didn't recognize. Bess introduced the older man as "Dear Peter," her fabulous gardener.

"He's unlike anyone I've had," said Bess. "He does all the weeding and keeps it all beautiful. Did you notice the roses? Best we've had for years."

Peter gave a toothy grin at this mention of himself. Anne gave Elaine a hug before seating herself. Elaine, (Anne knew from her previous visit) was about 15 years younger than Bess. A dedicated single woman, with short ginger colored hair, educated in London, and now teaching the students. Most of the students, eight to be exact, were young men who did not normally join to eat at the big house. They lived outside the complex and commuted in. The two female students, however, stayed in an apartment at the school, above the classrooms. These were the two young women at the table - now introduced as Kissa and Nasiche. Nasiche was quiet and reserved throughout the dinner. Apparently, the child was hers, and sat next to her in a high chair. Nasiche had the beautiful large lips and high cheekbones of an African queen. Kissa had a mischievous gleam in her eye, and her round face broke into a quick smile. Bess's other adopted daughter was referred to as Mila. Mila came from the kitchen and acknowledged Anne shyly, bending her slender neck with its head of curly hair. Both Mila and Joy served the food at a large counter – as Anne and the others filed by. Anne begged for a little less food on the plate, as the portions were extremely generous. *I certainly won't be a starving missionary here,* she thought. As though in response, Bess said "Don't expect such a feast every night. Some of us may be away to the villages or up north some evenings."

After Mila and Joy had joined the others at the table, Anna's hands were gripped by Peter's rough one and Joy's soft moist one on either side. Heads were bowed and grace was murmured by Elaine, in her low English accent. As they ate, the conversation turned to the day's doings. The new wing of the school needed painting, Bess commented, and she planned for the young men to stay after class an hour or two the coming week if Elaine could close lessons at three. Joy and Mila reported on a visit to a nearby village where they had distributed fruit to the poorest. One Muslim woman had accepted Christ.

"Did she know the danger from family?" asked Bess.

"Yes," responded Mila. "Her sister-in-law has recently converted and was with her, encouraging her. The sister-in-law's husband is also a Christian."

"They often keep it a secret," Bess said to Anne. "Some Muslims make a profession but then recant if family members find out. There is a danger from family and the new convert can be locked up or even killed." She sighed. "Ugandans are proud of their history of cooperation, but lately the extremists have become more numerous and influential."

Then to everyone, she added – "We'll put her on the prayer list and keep track of her. What is her name, Mila?"

"Sania," replied Mila.

Bess nodded. "It means 'radiant' in Arabic" she said to Anne.

Anne thought back to her tour of the big house three years ago. At the back of the pantry, hidden cleverly behind what looked like wooden shelving, was a hidden door made of steel. That door led into the "safe room." It was stocked with canned goods and necessities, and was there in case of a terrorist attack. In the twenty years Bess had lived here, Anne understood it had never been used.

Anne finished her meal of beef, beans, and well flavored greens. Desert was a superbly made upside-down cake. She was tired and her neck ached from the long flight out. As she relaxed, she took in the comfort around her. She loved the big house with its large kitchen and dining area. Through the hallway she glimpsed Bess's office, with its ponderous desk and mass of papers. Bookshelves covered the one visible wall. At the end of the dining room a picture of Bess hung on one wall. In a blue wrap, she looked somewhat severe. Another younger Bess in a framed photo sat on the carved cabinet next to Anne. It showed Bess leaning toward a man with dark hair. *He has a pleasant face,* Anne thought. She remembered that this was Bess's late husband. They had built and started the ministry together twenty years earlier. First the house was built, then the small school. The church came about some years later. The school was for seminary students, and Bess's husband was their teacher. Then seven years ago Bess's husband died suddenly. Anne remembered the story. He knew he was going – it was his heart - and he called for Bess. She knelt at his side on the floor and screamed for an ambulance. He commented on the severity of the pain, and then was gone. Bess had never really gotten over it. She was left with the hard decision of staying on at the mission and making a go of it without him, or returning to the States. She decided to stay and was eventually joined by Elaine. Bess treated the young seminary students as her children, and they in turn watched out for her. Anne turned her gaze to look with almost worshipful admiration at Bess.

Anne left the big house that evening and picked her way across the grass by means of a light on her phone, to her own quarters. She looked forward to tomorrow when she would begin her work. She would be joining Joy and Mila on a trip to a poor area nearby.

CHAPTER TWO

Though dead tired, for some reason Anne could not fall asleep. The strange environment and a dog barking in the distance kept her awake. Was it Sampson, the house dog? Anne's mind wandered back to the States. Before this trip, she had taught elementary school. She enjoyed working with students, though sometimes they engaged in such antics. But overall, she understood her fifth graders, with their changeable moods and the drama of their young lives. (Though when she was growing up, it didn't seem that hormones were as active as they were now-a days.) She related most especially to the shy and troubled kids. Jonathan, with his downturned eyes and feet that scuffled awkwardly around the others. Melissa, who kept her gaze averted as well and seemed lost in a world of her own. Yes, she cared about the children and was proud of her teaching degree. She was beginning to get the hang of it, but her idealism drove her to want to do more with her life.

Her apartment in Rio Rancho had been affordable, and large. That made up for the surrounding neighborhood, which was a barren looking, sandy lot. When the wind blew the sand ended up everywhere, even under the doorjambs.

Then three months ago, missionary Bess had sent out a plea to the church for someone to help teach and lead bible studies, asking for a two-year commitment. Room and board and a small stipend would be supplied. Eagerly, Anne expressed her interest. Having been to the compound before, she would be the perfect choice. She obtained references from her principle and assistant pastor. The main pastor of her church expressed concern that she was not ready for such an undertaking, but Anne dismissed his concern. It was a large church, and he didn't really know her, she reasoned. Anne ended up being accepted, though she never knew if there were any other applicants.

Anne reflected again on her previous trip to Uganda three years prior. She had stayed on Bess's compound at that time as well, but had been one of a team of eleven - six women and five men. They had all been housed above the school in two separate dormitory-style rooms – the men separate from the women. Bess had introduced the team to wealthier church members. Those Ugandans welcomed them into their homes, cooked for them, and took them shopping. The team visited various churches around Kampala and the surrounding area. Then of course there were the children, and the crusade. It was very exciting to be part of a crusade, as the church was able to hire a local Ugandan singer with his band. Two hundred people came forward, Anne was told later. She herself was sequestered with the children, but even from a distance away, the loud music blared out over the lot of vacant land, filled with big tents and plastic chairs. The children had come from everywhere, unaccompanied by adults, and it was difficult keeping them entertained for four long hours amid the hubbub. Finally, Anne released them to sit with the adults, and many left.

The best part of her visit (brought back vividly at dinner) were the evenings, when the team gathered around Bess's big table and shared their experiences of the day, and prayed together. All this fed Anne, and she sopped it up – the way a Ugandan might sop up their broth with a bit of chapati.

Coming home afterwards to the States and her roomy but lonely apartment could only be described as a shock. It was a though she returned to a world that valued materialism and status - one that she no longer embraced.

Anne sighed, and pulled the blanket up. She felt drowsy at last. As a young girl, she had read stories of everyday people who had given their lives in service to something greater than themselves, and now she was following in their footsteps. She closed her eyes and drifted off. There was no higher calling.

—

Morning dawned, the filtered light making its way into Anne's quarters. She lay awake on the bed, savoring the feeling of waking rested and refreshed. Outside she heard distant voices and male laughter. Then she wondered at the time and leaned over to check her cell phone. She had found an outlet the previous afternoon and the adapter had fit perfectly. It was now 6:30 am and breakfast was at 7:00. Jumping up, she tried the shower and learned why the shower curtain wasn't needed. The flow of water was a thin stream, pooling in the depression in the floor that was the shower basin. The hot water was non-existent. Perhaps there was a switch somewhere to start the boiler. Looking around she found it and switched it on, but knew it would take some time for the water to heat up. A cold shower would have to do today. Shivering, she toweled off and dressed hurriedly. In the hand mirror she had found in a drawer beneath the sink, she gazed at herself. Freckled face, light brown hair cut shoulder length, with bangs, eyes brown. She wrapped her hair up in a pony tail. She looked tired. Even at twenty-seven, she was no beauty, she decided. Some mascara on her light lashes would be an improvement, but she had made the decision not to bring any type of make-up. It didn't seem appropriate on the mission field.

Opening her door, she stepped out into the sunshine. Across the lawn she could see some young men over by the school along with the figures of Elaine and Bess. She made her way across to them and was introduced to students Dembe, Bitalo, Paul, Joseph, and Noah. Each in turn took her hand and shook it, saying "you are welcome." *How would she remember them all?* she wondered. Joseph was the tallest, and Bitalo had a bit of a squashed nose. Perhaps she should write their names down in her journal. There were three more students yet to arrive, but Bess encouraged her to go and have breakfast at the big house.

At the house, Anne found Mila and Joy there eating, the women students just leaving. Mila wanted to jump up and serve her, and Anne allowed her to, not wanting to be disrespectful, though she certainly could have served herself.

After thanking Mila, she asked "Where will we be going today?"

"Today we are going to Katanga," said Joy. "It is one of the slums of Kampala."

"Sounds great," said Anne.

Joy looked at her for a moment. "It can be difficult for some people to see."

Anne nodded, feeling slightly chastised.

The air was already feeling uncomfortably warm as the van rocked through Kampala, Devon once more at the wheel. The dirt road had not only ruts, but large holes that had to be avoided. The warming air made the trees shimmer.

Anne was curious because she had not been out to the poorer areas before. "What will we be doing?"

"Ministering to the needy," replied Joy. "We have pamphlets to hand out and are thinking of starting a bible study there."

The short grass was interspersed with taller bunches of another thick grass, more than ten feet high.

"What kind of plant is that"? asked Anna.

"That is Elephant grass" responded Joy. "And those are Acacia trees."

She pointed to scattered trees with wide elegant canopies. Anne could see they were covered with what looked like yellow flowers.

"They are beautiful and more plentiful in the hills" Joy added.

Anne looked around and could see the rolling hills in the distance. Somewhere not too far away was Lake Victoria.

As they continued, they began to see more trash along the roadside, and the buildings were more congested. Eventually the van pulled off into a more modest area. Driving slowly now along the narrow road, Anne saw Ugandans stare at her as they passed by. Finally, the van came to a stop and children gathered around the vehicle.

"Here they speak Luganda," said Joy, pushing some pamphlets into Anne's hand. "The children will greet you.

Then we will walk about. We will distribute mostly to women and the older children."

As they climbed down from the van, the children pressed in, and the body odor became overpowering. Mila didn't seem to notice it. She spoke to them, apparently asking them to wait their turn. Smiling, Anne greeted them. Each child knelt before her and shook her hand, murmuring "Gyebale ko Nnyabod". Anne nodded her head in return.

Mila spoke in her ear. "They are saying "Hello madam." You say "Ka JJambo" in return. That means a simple 'hi'."

The three women started down the streets and alleyways, handing out the pamphlets. Devon accompanied them, and Joy explained that it was always good to have a man with them as the slums were a dangerous place.

The area seemed a haphazard arrangement of broken-down homes. Some were made of timber and sheet metal; others of mud or concrete. Narrow alleyways crisscrossed so that Anne was sure she would be lost if on her own. But Devon seemed to have a perfect sense of direction. Everywhere, children sat or played. Women sat listlessly. Clothes hung to dry on makeshift lines. Trash was discarded and trampled in the mud. Joy spoke softly to a woman sitting on a concrete stoop, and pressed a pamphlet into her hand. Anne noticed that one of the woman's eyes was clouded blue with cataract. Another little boy around six years old gazed at them and Anne saw his hideous cleft palate, cutting through the upper lip to his deformed nose – something so easily corrected in the States. As Anne followed the others, handing out pamphlets and smiling, she realized that she had never seen such poverty. These people had absolutely nothing. Anne wondered how they could live. As Anne stepped across a rivulet of water and mud, she realized with a start that it was sewage. The discovery nauseated her. Another older boy with a bright smile stopped to have a prolonged conversation with Mila. Then he pointed out a building to their left.

"His family lives there" explained Mila. "He would like his mother to come to the bible study."

Crossing the pathway to the building they ducked inside and the bright sun was dimmed by the interior. There was a pot containing something, and several blankets in a corner. There on a blanket, sat an older woman. She looked too old to be the boys' mother, but they crossed to greet her. *Perhaps a grandmother?* thought Anne. Mila kept her gaze averted respectfully and spoke in a low tone of voice. The woman nodded, spoke, and held out her hand for the pamphlet, and then the women left.

Once outside, Mila said "She didn't really want it, as she said she is not a Christian, but she took it out of politeness."

"Is she, his grandmother?" asked Anne.

"No, she is his mother," said Mila. People here don't live as long. "Perhaps she will change her mind and come if we start a study."

The rest of the day was spent with the four making their way through the area, though at noon they took a break to sit in the van where there were bottles of water and sandwiches that had been packed away under the seat.

"Nothing ever tasted so good" said Anne gratefully. Joy smiled but said "don't let the children see you eating, because they will want some and we don't have enough for them all."

On the way back to the compound, Anne said to Mila "We must do more."

Anne thought that Mila would agree, as she seemed to have a tender heart, but she shook her beautiful head.

"Our resources are limited. If we give to one family, everyone will want the same, just like with the children. But we offer community and love, and hope they will learn about Jesus."

"But can they even read?"

"Many at Katanga can't. We pass out the pamphlets anyway, because some might read it, but we will return and we will invite them again to the bible study. We start music, and as people hear, they will come and hear the good news."

CHAPTER THREE

ON SUNDAY, THOSE FROM THE HOUSE, AS WELL AS THE seminary students gathered at the compound's church. When Anne had first arrived, she had seen it with the chairs stacked on the sides, but this morning it had been transformed. The students had lined up all the chairs, making an aisle down the middle. On one end of the church was a platform with a simple wooden podium and a drum set and amplifier.

As individuals began to gather, Anne saw that many people came from the surrounding area. Small families, dressed in their best sat on the flimsy chairs and laughed and talked to each other, leaning across the rows to shake hands with others. Men sat with their wives, and children sat on the laps of their mothers. As the music began, people stood and began to clap and sing loudly. Dembe was at the drums, and Bitalo led the music, alternating songs in English with those in the local language. Sometimes he sang a line, and then waited for the congregation to echo him. Whereas in the States, a congregation would sing three or four praise songs, here the music continued, each song building more enthusiastically, hands raised, bodies swaying. One woman sang out loudly from the congregation, at one point taking over from Bitalo in ecstatic praise. Then another man took over, bending his body forward in a dance in the aisle. Voices blended and harmonized. Some songs, though sung in Luganda were well known tunes to her. Others in English, she sang along with. At long last, Bitalo held up his hands and quieted the congregation. At this point Joseph stood up to preach. He praised the congregation and welcomed them. He pointed out several older individuals toward the back of the room who had come some distance to be with them. His preaching was simple and direct.

"We know Jesus" he said in his accented English. "But others do not."

Bitalo translated into the local language.

Joseph continued, "Who is going to tell them? If we see a man under a heavy load, will we not help him out and relieve his burden? Yes, we will. If we see a man dying because he does not know Jesus, will we not help also to relieve him of his burden? Yes, we will."

"Yes brother" said a man loudly.

"If we see a sister who is under a heavy burden, will we not help relieve her of her burden? Will we not tell her about Jesus?"

"Amen" said a woman in a pink flowered dress.

"And if we see a child" said Joseph, moving and putting his hand on the head of a youngster in the front row, "will we not welcome him as Jesus welcomed the little children"

"Mmmmm," agreed the congregation.

"And how can we expect Jesus to welcome us," Joseph went on, pointing upward, "unless we say in our hearts 'You are most welcome, Lord!'"

After the service there was the usual mingling, and Ann shook many hands, feeling as though she were a celebrity. Kissa grabbed her elbow and dragged her outside on the grass to play a game similar to duck, duck, goose, goose with the group of children. They giggled and raced around the circle, smiles wide. Anne was exhausted after being chosen multiple times to run. Having lost her shoe in some mud, she retrieved it and then stood watching, catching her breath. When a little boy in white trousers tugged on her to play again, she was saved, as his mother just then called out, "Isaza, time to go."

CHAPTER FOUR

Anne gathered routinely now in the church with the woman's bible study. The first afternoon Anne was to lead, the attendance was meager. Five came with their bibles. Three weeks later there were eleven women attending. All thankfully spoke English. Anne called the group "her" study, but that was a little possessive, because everyone was growing individually quite apart from her. The group was like a large Latana flower with its individual blossoms, Anne thought. There were now eleven women attending, and this afternoon, gaiety broke out in dancing. Ugandans sway and sing with natural rhythm and Ochen in her green skirt and short t-shirt shook her hips seductively as she made a slow circle. Then others joined in, singing and clapping, mirroring each other. Anne felt a light embarrassment. In Uganda only the areas below the waist were sexualized, yet this seemed the area most focused on in Ugandan dance. When everyone had worn themselves out and taken their seats, there was general chatter about the success of their beading projects. Violet proudly told of her sales that week and held up the beautifully beaded coin purse she had last finished. "Mum, is it not beautiful?" she asked, and Anne had to agree. The green and yellow were sown together intricately and the clasp done to perfection.

"Bible study first," said Anne. "And then we will work on our projects."

The afternoon progressed and the low murmuring of the

women was somewhat musical as they bent over their bibles to study John. The miracle in Cana of Jesus turning water to wine was well understood and conversation centered on the importance of the dignity of the bridegroom.

"The bridegroom would have been disgraced without the wine," said Ola.

"Jesus did right in listening to his mother as well," remarked Violet.

"What choice did He have?" interjected Nafuna. "She should have let Him be. Afterall, He said His hour had not yet come."

The compound had provided bibles and the women treated them as precious items. Today there were ten women present – Ayesha was missing, and Anne shrugged away a quick, sharp feeling of worry. She was not usually absent. Ayesha was a new convert - one of three Anne now knew of having converted from the Muslim faith. She wore the hijab while walking to the study, but once within the church she would discard it almost as if it were her private rebellion. She brought her baby Amina, that everyone adored and called "Nia." Ayesha was a young widow, living now under her brother's roof. Her brother knew of her conversion and disapproved but did nothing to dissuade her from the bible study.

As the study ended, the women pulled the long tables together and drew out their beads. Now they laughed again and spoke loudly and gossiped. Anne had yet to address the issue of gossip. They spoke of Jendyose's boyfriend Akpan.

"He is so shy" reported Ochen. "He's thinking he can marry her but is afraid to talk to the father. A marriage was arranged years ago, but she doesn't want to follow through.

She doesn't like the one they chose. He is fat. She wants Akpan. Can you believe how everyone feels? Of course, Jendoyose wants a Christian wedding but it costs too much."

"They should just get married in a church" interposed Nafuna, who was young and had her own ideas.

"No," said Miremba, a large stout woman. "It's legal, but not enough. And what about the bride price?" She closed her teeth and shook her head.

A woman in an orange dress changed the subject. "Did you know Sade's brother has HIV"?

"Didn't they know?" asked one of the ladies.

"No, he was never tested until recently. You wonder where he got it," said the lady in the orange dress.

"Well, he's a truck driver, isn't he? You **know** where he got it," said Ola.

"Eeee."

"You shouldn't talk that way, Ola, with so many of us struggling" reminded Beatrice. She was middle aged, dressed in a colorful dress with a sash wrapped around one shoulder.

"Did you hear Khalayi's cousin has become Christian?" asked Ochen again in the green. "But he has two wives so what is he to do? He can't abandon one."

"What should he do, miss Anne? The bible says to have only one wife."

This was more than Anne could answer. She shook her head.

"The first wife should stay," said Nafuna firmly, tossing her earrings.

"What do you know. You've only been married a year," said Miremba.

Some nodded and chuckled. Nafuna was newly married but proud of herself, and felt she had all the answers.

When the sun began to dip lower and shine under the large wooden doors, the women packed up to leave and assisted in moving the tables back.

"Read your bibles" reminded Anne as they left, "and we will meet again next week."

The doors closed leaving Ann in the large one-room church building to reflect on the day. She switched on the lights up by the ceiling. In Uganda electricity was spotty, though blessedly the compound had a back-up generator. Anne took her time stacking the plastic chairs back on the sides of the church, and sweeping the floor, retrieving stray beads and bits of fabric. She hummed lightly as she swept, thinking of the ladies. Violet was a delight, and Nafuna had so much enthusiasm.

The light had shifted again, and as the horizon raised a shoulder the sun dropped below it. Anne felt the cool of the evening beginning to steal over her. Dinner would be finished at the big house, but on bible study night Anne always ate in her own quarters.

Anne shuttered the side door when a small sound – a tap - came from outside and she re-opened the door. A black face shown at her under the hijab, the whites of the eyes glowing in the gloom. It was Ayesha and then Anne noticed that she clutched a bundle and was breathing quickly.

"Mum," said Ayesha imploringly.

Anne drew her inside and could see Ayesha's face – drawn and sweaty.

"Good heavens, what's wrong?" asked Anne.

Now Ayesha was speaking quickly – recounting her

flight from home. Her father had found out that she was now a Christian, and had locked her in the bedroom. But the baby had cried and cried until they had let her out to tend to Nia. She had been able to escape on pretense of gaining privacy to nurse the baby. She was running, but she knew not where. To friends. But the baby… She thrust it at Anne. Would Anne watch over the baby until she could come back?

Anne held the warm bundle, speechless for a moment, and then, "How long?"

"I don't know. As soon as I can find another place. A place that's safe."

"Come stay here, at the big house. You will be safe here," said Anne.

Ayesha was silent, but shook her head slightly.

"Please. Everyone will be glad to have both of you," she pleaded.

But Ayesha shook her head more decidedly and refused.

Anne sat in her quarters and held Nia close. Ayesha had slipped away into the night, leaving Anne staring after her into the dark. The tiny face had perfect features – the mouth like the pedals of a rose - the dark eyes looking out at Anne with an infant's serenity. Anne sighed. Soon the infant would need a feeding. She had found its diaper dry. It was a relief that the baby had a diaper, as many in Uganda were undiapered or wrapped in rags. Anne had found that out by holding an infant in Katanga.

Anne savored this moment, and that, she realized, was different. She was usually awkward around infants. She had never wanted children because she had always felt underneath some inadequacy regarding motherhood. In fact, she had had frightening dreams of having a child but forgetting to feed it, or forgetting where she had left it – as though it were a piece of baggage. Surely that did not bode well. But holding the baby brought a just noticeable stirring – as though there were a small seed within her ready to germinate. The thought of it was pleasant. She shifted Nia's weight, and took in the scent of her. But of course, she couldn't keep the baby here. She had to take it to the big house.

Here in Uganda, Anne was an oddity. She knew she was pitied because she had no husband or children. One day a child in a village had asked her why she had no husband, and had remarked matter-of-factly that she would be happy if she got one. Then the child had considered and said that if the husband gave her no children, Anne should get rid of him and get another. Only Beatrice in the bible study seemed to have a different opinion. Beatrice had been widowed by the death of her husband many years ago. Her one son was now in college, and apparently it had been a hard road for Beatrice as a single mother. Anne knew that widowed women were frequently thrown out by the late husband's family, and left homeless and without resources, and when Anne told her she had no children and was unmarried, Beatrice had nodded and said "maybe that's a good thing."

Anne entered the porch area of the big house, almost stumbling over the shoes piled to the side. She knocked rather than entering, as the dining area appeared dark. Joy opened the door to her and stood gaping at the baby in Anne's arms. A few moments later Bess had been called, then Mila and finally Elaine. The women all stood surrounding her, listening carefully to Anne's story of Ayesha. Anne could tell by the set of Bess's jaw that she was not pleased, but that something had to be done.

"Mila," Bess said, "go see if Nasiche is in the apartment. She may have extra bottles and diapers."

The big house was abuzz that evening with the coming of the baby. Nasiche brought over a bottle, some used clothing, and diapers that were a little large for the tiny infant. Nia was passed around, and the young women exclaimed over her, though Anne could tell that Bess and Elaine were tense. They spoke quietly to each other, away from the others, and Anne caught Elaine eyeing her.

Later when they were standing together, Elaine spoke. "It was not wise to bring the baby here. Bess is worried."

Anne shook her head, uncomprehending.

"Don't you see," said Elaine. "What if Ayesha's father finds out the baby is here and that we've assisted Ayesha. What if he is well connected?"

The next few days passed as usual, though Anne found more time to spend with Nia, who was now in Joy and Mila's care. Mila normally cared for Nasiche's son Gabriel when Nasiche was in class. Over the last two days Ayesha had not been seen, and had not come back for the baby. On the third day at noon all were seated at the table having finished eating. Bess was discussing with Devon a problem with the van's brakes, and the cost of having that repaired. There was nothing to be done – the van would have to be taken to the shop. Mila then interrupted the gathering to report that the baby was eating poorly and now seemed to be running a sudden temperature. As she held the baby, they gathered around and looked at the tiny body. Anne could see a twinge of yellow in the skin, and the breathing was rapid.

"Other symptoms?" Bess asked.

"She is drowsy," said Mila, "but won't sleep."

Bess came to a quick decision. "Take her now to the hospital clinic. Go with Devon."

"What is wrong?" asked Anne.

"She may have malaria" replied Bess.

Anne was aghast. May I attend?" she asked.

Bess nodded her head. "Go with them" she said.

The hospital clinic was not far, and as Devon looked for a better place to park the car, Mila carried Nia in with Anne following. They accepted the infant immediately and took her behind closed doors. Mila was allowed inside, but Anne was left standing in the lobby. After a short time, Mila came out and told Anne the doctors had started an IV and were giving medication. She would stay with the baby, but perhaps Anne would like to walk around the grounds. Anne could pray for the patients, but wasn't to go into building 5 as that was for those with Tuberculosis.

Obediently Anne walked out onto the grounds. The clinic was made up of separate numbered buildings and as Anne walked by the first one, she could hear loud voices. Peeping through the doorway, she saw a group of men. Between two she saw a quick glimpse of a man who looked like he had a machete embedded in his skull. He was being held down, but apparently was wide awake, and cursing. Anne withdrew quickly and hurried on to the next building. Here the large room was filled with two rows of metal beds, with an aisle between. Anne smiled as well as she could at one man who was awake, and asked him if he would like prayer.

"What can I pray for?" she asked.

The man put his hand on his chest, and Anne decided it might be his breathing. He nodded an affirmative and Anne stood near the head of his bed and prayed. Anne went down the line of beds, praying for some that were awake, though others declined or did not seem to speak English.

After this, Anne went on to another building that apparently housed burn victims. They lay piteously on their beds. There was the smell of rotting flesh, and Anne had courage to pray for only one before moving on.

Outside she saw another building with two women sitting outside.

She sat beside one and said "Hello. My name is Anne. Would you like prayer?"

At that moment, Anne heard Mila over at the edge of the building. She called out "come away," and gestured for Anne. Surprised, Anne left the woman and met Mila.

"They have TB," explained Mila.

"Oh no." Anne's face was ashen. She looked up and saw the number 5 plainly above the doorway.

"I can't believe I did that. Do you think I'll contract TB?"

"You will be ok," said Mila. "Exposure has to be longer."

Before leaving the hospital, Anne was allowed to see Nia briefly. The little body looked frail and helpless, with an IV attached to a vein in her tiny head. There was no improvement yet, they were told, and they were advised to leave and come back the next day.

That evening Anne felt plagued with guilt, thinking of Nia. She should have insisted that Ayesha take Nia with her. Anne sank to her knees beside the bed and prayed. Tears stung her eyes and she poured out her heart and reminded God of the innocent life that needed His healing. Jesus had cared for the little children. Surely God would watch over Nia and keep her safe. As she prayed, she sensed a peace come over her, and felt assured that God had heard and was answering.

Hours later Anne awoke cramped and cold in the same position she had been kneeling in. Climbing into the bed, she again heard distant barking, followed this time by answering dogs.

The situation with Nia was unchanged for the next few days. On the third day news came that Nia had died, despite the infusion of Artesunate. Bess sat with folded hands at the table, her fingers and arms bleached white by the morning sun.

Ayesha had also been found. She had been beaten savagely and left on the streets. Sometime later it appeared a pack of wild dogs had gotten to her.

Anne's eyes were dry, but she felt as though she had slipped into a dark well of numbness, with her faith left glittering above like fool's gold.

CHAPTER FIVE

On the day after being informed of the deaths of Ayesha and Nia, Anne sat out under a gazebo on the lawn. The light flickered through the slatted roof and made a pattern of intersecting triangles on the grass. Anne felt a heaviness that was difficult to shake. Sampson lay beside her, and she absently combed her fingers through his shaggy hair. He maneuvered his body so that he could put his large wet snout on her leg, and looked at her dolefully, as though reading her mood. At least he was not blaming her, she thought. Not that the others were really blaming her, she acknowledged, but there was an air of dampened energy on the compound.

She felt disconnected. Her mind wandered and she thought of her childhood. She could identify a lifetime of loneliness. Her family was broken from the effects of alcoholism. Left to care for herself in many ways, she had drifted. Consequently, her employment history had been one of short-term menial jobs. Back then it was more comfortable to keep running – never allowing anyone to really know her. But then one day she had accepted Jesus and He had given her new life. It sounded so cliché, but it was true. The event was still bright in her memory. At the church service the pastor talked about the heavy burden of sin so many carried. It was obvious to Anne as he spoke, that her life felt like a heavy burden. When the pastor asked "who is tired of trying to live life on their own terms and in their own strength? Who needs a savior?" Anne saw her life with clarity. She had lived, yet not really lived. She had always avoided others. How was it possible to be so self-sufficient, and yet at the same time feel desperately needy? Only because the self-sufficiency was an act. She had perfected a mask to hide the neediness, but the fact was, she was tired of pretending. Sitting there, eyes closed, she knew the pastor saw through everything and was speaking directly to her. In that moment, she was sure that if she opened her eyes, he would be looking directly at her – his eyes boring into hers. When he offered Jesus as the Way the Truth and the Life, and asked people to come forward, she knew she needed Jesus. As the music swung into gear, she accepted Jesus, publicly making her way down the aisle. In that moment she felt a relief and connection she had never felt before. The angels exulted. Looking back now, she could say it was the biggest moment of her life, and had given her the security and determination to attend college and major in education. It had also been the impetus for her first trip to Uganda.

As Anne rubbed Sampson's head, a new determination took hold of her. It was not a letting go, but self-effort taking hold, though Anne didn't know it. She was only determined to make a difference where she was in Uganda.

Anne begged Bess to let her go out to the poor areas of Kampala herself, taking Devon with her to translate. Over the next several weeks she visited various poor settlements. She returned frequently to Katanga, and tried to get to know the residents – especially the older woman they had passed a pamphlet to on Anne's first visit. She found that the woman's name was Fatuma, and her 11-year-old son, Adroa. Adroa had eyes like melting chocolate, and he would sit nearby listening to the conversation. Fatuma had been convinced by him to attend Joy and Mila's bible study one time, but she had remained uncommitted and had not returned. Fatuma had some type of deformity to her leg and could not walk easily, and on her third visit, Anne saw an old wheelchair beside the building that apparently Adroa would use to take his mother around the village. As Anne began visiting regularly, Fatuma opened up and told Anne of her troubles. She was bitter, but who wouldn't be? Fatuma wanted her son to attend school, but had no money to pay. Her husband was an alcoholic and came home rarely. Anne felt sympathy, and began bringing the family a small amount of money each time she came. She would unwrap it and place it in Fatuma's outstretched hand. Anne knew Mila and Joy would not approve of the money, nor would Bess, so she didn't mention it. Devon didn't approve either, but he kept his mouth closed in a tight line. Perhaps, Anne thought, if she could just help a little with Adroa's schooling…

Often on returning from her frequent visits to Katanga, Anne felt disgust at the awful conditions she observed. Part of her wanted to hold in her arms every child, and part of her wanted to run from it.

Anne also spent any free time she had in learning Luganda. Though English and Swahili were the official languages of Uganda, around Kampala, the poorer people spoke Luganda.

One evening Bess met her as she came into the compound, dusty and worn from a long day. Bess looked her over with sharp eyes.

"I think you're doing too much" she told Anne, but Anne shrugged her off.

There was now a subtle feeling within Anne – a slight distaste when she thought of the privilege of the compound, and Bess's rule over it. *Shouldn't a missionary identify more with those she was trying to reach?* she thought. *Could they truly minister to the poor when they were walled up away from them?* Rebellion stirred quietly within her.

Because of her busy schedule, Anne was somewhat unwilling to take a holiday when Bess announced it, but it seemed she had no choice. Bess now had the van fixed and wanted to try it out. She had also received some money from a church in the states that helped support the compound and school. Therefore, Bess suggested they celebrate and take the seminary students to Lake Victoria for the day, followed by shopping downtown.

The morning was bright as they all moved towards the gate, the path passing by Peter's garden area. The avocados were being harvested and Anne could see where some had already fallen to the ground. Peter offered her one and she held it in her palm and felt its heaviness. It fit in her whole hand with its outstretched fingers. Anne could also see rows of some type of unknown greens – as well as what she identified as beets, carrots, and corn with its stalks and husks rising above her head. These were the fresh vegetables that fed them in the evenings. She thanked Peter for the avocado, and the group climbed into the van. The engine idled. Nasiche was allowed to stay home today with Gabriel, and wouldn't be joining them, but everyone else was included. The seminary students were as excited as children going on a field trip, their smiles contagious. The three male students Anne had not met initially were named Dejen, Andrew, and Ade.

"Where is Noah?" asked Elaine. Everyone looked back towards the school, and Bess appeared exasperated.

"Five more minutes" she said. Then we'll leave without him. Joseph, go get him."

But at that moment everyone saw Noah running from the doors across the grass to the van. With his long gait it was more of a bounding lope. As he grabbed the rail and swung up on the steps, Bess began a little tune in a sing-song voice. It was the same melody as Frere Jacques, only with different words.

The others joined: "You've been primping, you've been primping; now you're late, now you're late; hurry up and find a seat, hurry up and find a seat; we won't wait, we won't wait."

They laughed. Noah's mature face flushed under his black skin, and he slid into a seat toward the back.

Anne felt both protective towards him and slightly resentful. How often had she been teased in her lifetime? In fact, not only teased, but bullied. Bess demanded promptness, but Anne had learned that in the Ugandan culture, any set time was an estimate at best. Surely, she was being too hard on him, singing that ridiculous song as though he were a child.

The lake was a little more than an hour away, and as the van bounced along, the students bounced along with it with Kissa and Paul singing "the wheels on the bus go round and round," and "the people on the bus go sweat, sweat, sweat," until Elaine said she couldn't take any more verses. Finally, they pulled into the parking area of a resort that had beautifully manicured landscaping. Shortly after, they boarded a ferry. The flat ferry boat had lines of seats, and everyone chose their places. Then off they went, puttering away, the motor whining, as though it could use a little grease.

The water was a brownish green and the ferry maneuvered and kept as close to the shore line as possible to view the wildlife. Alex, both driver and tour guide, was small and wiry, his brown hands moving quickly to steer and shift gears. At times he would shut off the motor and let the boat rest in the quiet of the lake. At those times Anne could already feel the heat rising from the water and deck and was grateful for her long shirt sleeves which were protection from the flies and mosquitoes.

Now Alex turned off the motor and pointed to the shore. As they floated closer, everyone gathered on that side of the boat to see a four-foot monitor lizard with its heavy body and short legs. Its claws dug deeply into the dirt as it shifted but stayed its ground defiantly. Its long-forked tongue licked out at them. Along the shore Anne could see what looked like crabs, and some large fish swam by. Alex described the fish as Nile perch – mild in flavor and good for eating. As the boat's motor started up again, Alex reversed, and then set them on course again. Ann was grateful for the moving air that dispelled the stagnant feel of the lake.

After some time passed, Alex gave a shout and all looked over to where he now steered the boat. A group of hippos could be seen with their eyes and nostrils showing above the water. They bobbed up and down, and Alex said they were sleeping. What funny big eyes, Anne thought. As the boat motored by, Anne suddenly saw two hippos erupt from the water and race for shore, their ponderous bodies moving swiftly, the water flung from their glistening hides. It was as though their weight propelled them forward.

"They seldom move that fast," said Alex excitedly. "It could be a crocodile, but hippos don't normally feel threatened by them. I think they may be playing."

On shore the hippos had stopped and stood still. Anne watched. "How fun," she thought, but no further action occurred. As the boat moved off, she saw them lay down in the dirt.

Not long after, Joseph pointed toward the center of the lake and shouted "crocodile!" Anne hurried to look, but all she could see was a dark long shadow, perhaps ten feet long, passing swiftly along. It made Anne think of sea monsters.

The boat ride was fascinating, and Anne began to enjoy it despite her best intentions not to. She saw occasional monkeys in the trees. They moved quickly on the far shore, swinging away from sight in the blink of an eye. Anne looked more intently at what appeared to be a monkey stuck lifelessly in the branches. When Anne asked Alex, he shrugged and said he guessed it had just died. Anne wondered to herself if the animal would simply decompose where it was. The thought emerged, "Someone should take it down." Though Anne didn't voice it, she was aware of the difference between her American sensibilities and those of the Ugandans.

As the ferry neared the apex of the lake, Anne could hear a distant roar, and as they rounded a bend, the Victoria Falls came into view. Alex kept the boat at a distance with some difficulty, as now the water was pushing against them.

Anne wished they could be closer and experience the rush and excitement of the water. She recalled a small waterfall that as a child, she had been able to get behind, and how it had pounded on her as she swam out.

"This," Alex said proudly, "is the world's greatest sheet of falling water."

Anne believed him as she viewed the violent cascade and the spray that spread like a hazy cloud surrounding it. Even from this distance it was impressive.

"The spray creates mist and rainbows," said Alex.

On the trip back, the wind was against them and cooled the air greatly, providing relief. Even the mosquitos seemed to give up and disappear. Several students had phones with cameras and Kissa preened and posed in front them with various students. She wore a fashionable jumper suit in summer green. Anne was grabbed and made to pose with her, and Anne laughed, feeling a sudden lightness of heart.

During the ride, Alex gave more information about the lake. It was shared by Kenya, Tanzania, and Uganda. On the northern side the lake touched the line of the equator. Lake Victoria was the largest tropical fresh-water lake in the world. Alex pointed to the distance and indicated that in that direction, the lake eventually emptied into the White Nile.

"The Nile" Alex explained, "is the only river that runs from south to north, away from the equator, before emptying into the sea."

That was curious. "It's as though it were running uphill," Anne thought to herself.

Off to one side, Anne could see an island.

"Is that island meaningful?" she asked.

"That is Musambwa island," said Alex. "It is a safari site. Musambwa means 'gods' or 'spirits. The spirits there take the form of snakes. There are 2,000 snakes on the island," he said proudly. "Also, many species of birds."

As he steered closer, Anne could see the rocky landscape broken by bushes and twisted Ficus trees. The trees were so bent, some of the branches dipped down into the water.

"It is said that 100 men live on the island, but no women. Legend says that if anyone has sex, the gods will humiliate whoever it is. Therefore, men must go to the main land for that."

Anne saw Kissa roll her eyes.

But Bess said, "It is true that there is a very low rate of HIV and sexually transmitted diseases on the island."

"What type of snakes?" asked Anne.

"Many kinds" replied Alex. "Many cobras and vipers."

Anne shuddered, thinking that she would decline a visit if offered.

Following the ferry ride, there was a fancy lunch buffet at the resort. This was a treat, especially enjoyed by Mila and Joy who didn't have to cook. The air conditioning was a welcome relief, and the tables were set with white napkins beneath sparkling silverware. Everyone lined up with their plates, heaping them full. Laughter and gaiety pervaded the grand room with its view of the lake.

After lunch everyone piled back into the van to visit a tourist area for shopping. After parking, they walked along the streets which were set up with small booths and tables. A young man with a basket of green bananas pestered them until Joseph shooed him away. Shops also lined the roads with colorful clothing, beadwork, and even paintings displayed outside. Kissa wanted to buy some fabric to make a skirt, and everyone scattered in different directions. Joseph was with Anne to make sure she was charged fairly, though she was sure it was not necessary. She told him she didn't want anything, but nevertheless he led her from booth to booth, pointing out the bargains. At each, the proprietor would indicate the fine workmanship, and Anne would agree that it was very fine work. One large six-foot painting of a horse was especially focused on, and Anne nodded, admiringly. To herself she laughed, thinking that in her quarters she had no room to hang anything, much less a six-foot painting. They walked on. She almost wondered if Joseph were a friend of some of the vendors, trying to help them make a sale. Finally, Anne bought a small beaded coin purse, and a necklace crafted out of paper beads. Joseph at that point appeared satisfied that she had obtained things of value. Shortly after, they met back up with everyone else, and there was an admiring of Anne's coin purse and necklace, Kissa's fabric in bright orange and purple, and the pair of bookends Elaine had bought carved in the form of Elephants. Following this, they all together entered a dimly lit store that reminded Anne of an old five and dime in the states, and bought bags of chips and snacks for the trip home, though Anne couldn't image being hungry after the lunch they had eaten. Noah asked for money for a coke and chips, which Anne was happy to provide.

Elaine, however, scolded him, asking "where is your own money?"

The ride back was uneventful. Anne was relieved when they arrived back on the compound, and she could escape to her quarters and the company of her own thoughts. She set the coin purse on the table, removed her shoes, and sank down onto the bed. The trip had been fun, but she recalled a conversation she had had with Elaine on the Ferry. She had mentioned to Elaine that one of the young ladies in her bible study had asked for money - 20,000 shillings to buy new reading glasses, as she rolled over on hers in the bed and broke them. (Anne had given Nafuna the money, but didn't tell Elaine that.) Elaine had asked "how old is she?" and Anne responded, "Maybe in her twenties." Elaine had looked at Anne squarely. "Do you think a twenty-something year old would need reading glasses?" Anne had thought about it, but made no answer. "She probably saw a pair in the church up by the podium and wanted a pair," Elaine had concluded.

Anne sighed. Elaine seemed to be suspecting the worst of people. Anne dismissed the conversation and focused on the future. Tomorrow, she would return to Katanga. Fatuma had seemed more needy and depressed this last week. If only Anne could do more – give more of herself. If only she could bring Fatuma and Adroa here and house them in her own quarters. Compared to what they were used to, her own modest quarters were a palace. If only the big house could be used for such a thing. But of course, Bess would never allow any of it.

CHAPTER SIX

THE FOLLOWING WEEK, ANNE AND DEVON MADE THEIR way to Katanga. Anne gazed with interest out the window of the van. In some places she noted small plots of land cultivated with corn or other vegetables. She had learned that these plots, often between buildings, were claimed by whoever could get there first and cultivate it. There didn't seem to be much in the way of property lines. At almost every corner, boda-boda drivers waited for customers. Many seemed to be lounging – leaning against doorways or seated by the road. Though the motor bikes were really only to have one customer, sometimes they were loaded with as many as three family members behind the driver. One boda driver rode by with a load of vegetables. Another had wood balanced precariously, sticking out about four feet on either side. Everywhere people sat, walked, bicycled, waited. It was a place of communal living. *Such a crowded, poverty-stricken country,* thought Anne. Yet, everyone extended a certain graciousness and privacy. If someone urinated in the road, others would look away. At least the squat toilets were the norm. These were but a simple hole in the ground, set behind some type of wall for privacy, and often shared by more than one family. The fancy ones were tiled, but they were rare and reserved for tourists.

A woman walked on the side of the road with a large basket-full of fruit on her head. What amazing poise and balance she had. A group of men pretended to be filling in pot holes in the road, but Anne had learned from Devon that most pot holes didn't get fixed because when they were bad enough the government gave money. The van rocked around a corner and Devon took a cigarette out of his mouth and hung out the window, yelling at another driver. The cigarette was a rare luxury, and Anne seldom saw Devon smoke, but it seemed to put him in a talkative mood.

"You must be an aggressive driver to get anywhere," he said.

Anne nodded.

"There are no rules," he continued. "You just have to get your front bumper in front of the other guy. Then you've won."

He gave a slight chuckle, as though pleased that he had just won a round.

"In America if you drive straight, you're sober and if you weave, you're impaired. In Uganda you weave to avoid potholes if you're sober, but plow on straight if you're impaired."

"How do you know about America?" asked Anne.

"Missionary Bess has told me," Devon replied. He thought a moment. "You are very lucky to be rich and live in America, miss Anne."

"How do you know I'm rich?" asked Anne, slightly perturbed.

"White people are all rich," confided Devon. "Everyone here would like to be sponsored by a mzungu. Then they can be supported for life."

"What is a mzungu?"

"A white person."

Devon turned left at the next corner. "Another thing, miss Anne" he said.

Anne looked over at him.

"In case you're ever out by yourself and are lost, never ask for directions from a Ugandan."

"Why?" asked Anne.

"Because Ugandans don't like to disappoint you, so if you ask for directions and they don't know, they will give you directions anyway. They'll be wrong, but it will make you happy at the time."

He gave her a wry smile, and Anne wasn't sure if he was just having fun with her or not.

The van pulled into the Katunga that Anne now knew so well, and came to a stop. Anne grabbed her hat. This time Devon led the way by another route, and they stopped to pray with two women. Anne had half a dozen beaded bracelets that she gave out, the colors describing the salvation story. Anne asked a young woman who was sitting alone if she would like to hear the salvation story, and what the beads symbolized, and the woman nodded. At this, Anne described how the black bead represented our sin, the red - the blood of Jesus to make atonement for us, the yellow for the sunshine of the Spirit, and the green for the growth of a believer. When she finished, the woman thanked her. Devon spoke a bit more to the woman, and then told Anne that she was already a believer, but had wanted to hear the story anyway and know about the bracelet. Anne smiled at herself because of her own enthusiasm. Then she gave the woman a bracelet. Perhaps the woman would use it to share the story with others.

Tin walls glinted in the sun as they made their way

down a narrow pathway, stepping around mud puddles. Eventually Anne recognized where they were. They were near Fatuma's home.

"Let's visit Fatuma" Anne suggested.

They approached the building, and ducked inside. Stepping in from the bright sunlight to the shaded interior, it took Anne a moment for her eyes to adjust. Then she saw something she had not seen before. Beer cans littered the floor. Fatuma was asleep on a mattress next to the wall. Adroa was bending over a bucket of water, his bare back turned toward them. In the gloom Anne could still see the unmistakable marks of a beating. Hearing them approach, he turned his back away and faced them. Anne saw an emptiness in his eyes for the first time. Turning him around, she looked at his back. Savage red marks ran across his shoulders. There were also scars from previous beatings.

"Devon!" Anne exclaimed. "His father has come back and beat him."

Devon stilled her with his hand, and spoke gently to Adroa, leading him away a few steps. Anne could only understand a few words, but Adroa nodded towards his mother, talking rapidly to Devon. Devon came back to Anne and addressed her.

"It is not his father that beats him," he said. "It is his mother."

"But the alcohol – the beer cans," said Anne, confused. "His father is an alcoholic."

"Apparently it is she who drinks." Devon spoke again to the boy, and then reported to Anne "His father has not been in his life for many years."

Anne was dumbfounded and practically stuttered.

"B-but Fatuma said..." She caught her breath. "She lied? Why didn't Adroa say anything? And what about the money? I've given it for his schooling."

This time Devon had a more prolonged conversation with Adroa, and then turned back sadly to Anne.

"His mother has used the money on alcohol. The boy hoped that your visit would make her want to become a Christian, but he says it has not helped."

Adroa had slipped his shirt back on. Anne realized now that Fatuma was not asleep, but passed out from drunkenness.

"Surely he can't stay here," said Anne.

Again, Devon conversed with the boy, gesturing to the room and Fatuma. The boy shook his head vigorously. Devon addressed Anne again.

"He says he must stay with her. He is all she has. But he said that he will stay further away from her so as not to be beaten. She beats him when she is drunk and he is asleep. But only when she is able to buy alcohol."

Feeling dazed, Anne left the building with Devon, at a loss to know what to do. Her mind was spinning, but one thing was clear: She was a fool, giving Fatuma money every week, thinking it was used for Adroa's education. Her stomach sickened at the thought. Devon now turned his gentle voice to her, as though he were reading her mind. He spoke as he had spoken to the boy.

"Some people will change, but others will not. Some Ugandans have pride, others do not."

Anne felt indescribably weary and asked to be taken back to the compound. In the van she sighed and muttered aloud, "How does anyone get out of such a place?"

Devon was silent for a long time.

Then he responded with meekness, “Some of us do.”

“Some of you?” asked Anne.

Slowly the realization dawned on her. She recalled how Devon knew every path and house in Katunga -every twist and turn. Though the area stretched over at least a mile, he was never lost.

“You came from this place?”

Devon spoke quietly. “This was my home until I was eight. My parents were away a lot, and one day never came home. Perhaps it was a factory explosion that happened nearby.” He paused. “Missionary Bess found me and took me to a Christian orphanage and they educated me. She was my sponsor. Later when I was old enough, she hired me to drive for her.”

“Missionary Bess” repeated Anne.

“Yes, she is good to all of us. She took in her adopted daughters also. When Joy’s mother died of HIV, Missionary Bess took her in. Joy was also born with HIV. But because of the treatment, she is doing very well.”

“Joy has HIV?” asked Anne, incredulous, thinking of the beautiful young woman.

Devon nodded.

“And Bess has paid for the treatment?”

“Oh yes.”

On the way back to the compound, Anne struggled to reconcile herself with the new information. It was as if the world had shifted and tilted now at a strange angle; and everything rotated around her new feelings of guilt. She had provided money to someone and promoted alcoholism and abuse. She had dismissed Bess and did her a great disservice.

She had thought Bess didn't care. Not only that, but she had let her own ego take over and had played God. She had thought she could make changes that others couldn't – that she possessed the charity others didn't, when in fact she knew nothing. What did she know about this culture or these people? She couldn't even speak the language. Then the greatest blow of all came to her – what if God hadn't called her to this ministry at all? She pushed the thought away and focused on the present, but the bright sunny day had faded.

Over the next several weeks, Anne stopped pushing herself. She went through the motions, and tried to speak to people the way she had before, but it was as though she had sunk down into a pool of despondency. Everything seemed to take effort. Nafuna, who had borrowed money for reading glasses, continued to come to the bible study group, but without the glasses. Anne felt too tired to pursue the question and the young woman never offered an explanation. Anne realized that what Elaine had once said was true – Ugandans increased the price of things ten times for whites. It was not an exaggeration. Anne now appreciated Joseph's presence with her when she shopped. She once thought he was only there to translate, but now she knew he was with her to keep her from being unfairly charged. The whole relationship between Ugandans and money was clearer to her now. She once had the idea that Ugandans were untainted by the materialism of the States – and they were, in a sense – but they weren't as interested in money only because most of them didn't have it. Greed was universal. Stealing, she found, was also something shared.

One day she left her cell phone on the seat of the van while running into a store to buy some bobby pins. When she came out, it was gone.

Elaine explained that smart phones were very popular, but hard to come by. "You shouldn't even hold one out the window to take a photo because someone might grab it from you," she said.

With some difficulty, and Joseph's help, Anne was able to replace her phone with a less expensive model.

Anne spent more time with Beatrice, the older woman in her bible study. From visiting, Anne learned more about the death of Beatrice's husband who had been crushed under heavy equipment. With her son away in college, Beatrice made ends meet by translating occasionally for Bess, and doing laundry for other women. Beatrice had a solidness about her, Anne thought, in body and mind. She also had a calming effect on Anne. When Anne told her of the situation with Fatuma, Beatrice said little, but Anne felt the older woman instinctively understood.

One afternoon Anne went with Beatrice to assist a young woman named Maria who had a new baby. Anne hadn't ridden a Boda-Boda before, but she gamely followed Beatrices lead. The van was back in for repair, and Devon had taken the daughters out in the car. She seated herself carefully behind the driver, side-saddle, tucking her skirt beneath her and between her knees. Her Boda followed Beatrice's as they wove through town. Passing the prison, she saw men out in yellow and orange clothing working the ground. The colors signified those remanded (yellow) and those convicted (orange).

The ride was somewhat harrowing and Anne was

grateful when they pulled up finally to a stop and she could disembark, paying her man 5,000 shillings.

The home was built of cement block, with four rooms. The dirt floor was swept clean, and everything put in order. In the back room was Maria's husband, and they were introduced briefly. Outside, Beatrice pointed out the casava plants which were almost ten feet high.

"We will help by harvesting and cooking some casava for Maria" she said. They approached with a shovel and knife. "Here, you see it is ready to harvest because of the yellowing of the lower leaves," said Beatrice. "We cut it off a foot from the ground."

Beatrice demonstrated, throwing the top portion of stem and leaves into a pile off to the side.

"Then we pull the roots up."

Beatrice grunted with the effort and Anne assisted in loosening the roots with the shovel. After working for some time, Anne felt the sweat dripping down the front of her neck and chest.

"There," said Beatrice finally. That is enough. "Now we cut it up."

Sitting in two chairs on the back porch, Anne and Beatrice peeled and cut the root into small pieces. Then they boiled it in a large pot of water.

"You must boil it well," said Beatrice. "Otherwise, it is poisonous."

After boiling until it was tender, Beatrice mashed the root, and then they left it for Maria.

"That will help her," said Beatrice. "She will fry it up for dinner. That's the best way to cook it. Otherwise, it tastes like chalk dust to me."

Saying goodbye, they left. Indeed, Maria was very grateful.

Walking away, Anne asked Beatrice "Why doesn't her husband help her with the farming?"

"Farming is woman's work," said Beatrice. "Men don't normally cultivate the ground except at the prison."

"So, what does he do?" asked Anne.

"He can afford to sit at home because they have some money," said Beatrice. "In Uganda, woman do most of the work." She thought a moment. "The women carry Uganda on their backs."

CHAPTER SEVEN

THEY HUDDLED BEHIND THE METAL DOOR, DOWN FOUR steep steps in the safe room. They were all still in a tight wad of fear – the four young Ugandan women, Bess, Elaine, Anne, Peter, and Devon. Sampson lay on the floor, in the corner. Everyone practically held their breaths for as long as they could, and when they had to breathe, it was done shallowly, taking in portions of dust, as though shallow breathing would be quieter.

The darkness was broken only by a small area of filtered light that came through a grated window in the middle of the far wall. It illuminated some shelving and canned as well as dry goods. The light made the dust visible. Now, on the other side of the door, in the house, they could hear distant crashes, as if crockery were being smashed, or chairs broken. Muted shouts in another language – Arabic? – could be heard, as the invaders focused on the kitchen. Mila murmured to Sampson soothingly and stroked his coat with her slender fingers. Anne and the others each prayed silently that they would not be discovered. As they waited it sounded as though the disrupters had moved out of the kitchen, into other rooms. Everyone breathed a little more deeply, and Anne sat, her back against a shelf. The smell of dust and of dried beans and of general mustiness came to her nostrils. For a moment she thought she would sneeze, but graciously the urge passed. Imaginations flittered off in different directions – Elaine's to the school, Bess's to her home, Peter's to the garden. Anne thought back to Ayesha and Nia. Everyone feared the worst.

* * *

The morning after Nia's death, Bess and Anne had contacted the women they could reach from the bible study, and asked whether any knew Ayesha's full name or where she lived with her brother. No one knew. Violet wondered if it might be the area near the Kibuli mosque, which was nearby.

Joseph and Devon set out, with Anne (as she would not be left behind). They scoured the area, starting near the Kibuli mosque. They made inquiry discretely for Ayesha or her brother. Some people did not respond, others shook their heads. Anne felt that many were looking at her curiously. One man's response seemed promising as he said he knew an Ayesha. He appeared interested and asked where they were from. Joseph explained they were from the Christian compound. At this the man seemed to shut down, and turned away.

One brown skinned man with a pock-marked face was listening to the conversation, but he only gave them a blank stare. As they walked away, Anne turned to see him still looking at them. Then he moved quickly behind some buildings.

The day grew hot as the afternoon waned. They returned to the area around the Kibuli mosque, and heard the late afternoon call to prayer through the loud speaker like some bestial wail. The mosque sat on a hill and the low sun shone on its dome and the I around its arched doorways.

The search ended up being unfruitful, and they returned to the compound to report a lack of success.

Everyone was subdued at dinner, but after the dishes were taken away and washed, Bess seemed to have come to a decision. "We must bury the infant" she said. "The Muslim tradition is to bury the dead within twenty-four hours." The infant was wrapped in a white cloth, and before the evening sun set, the inhabitants of the big house gathered at the small cemetery on the property. This area was set apart on the south side. It was pretty, Anne thought. It was shaded by rosebushes. Peter used a spade to dig the small hole in the moist earth. Not far away was Bess's own husband. No coffin was used for Nia, as per Islam tradition. However, Bess used a Christian prayer, commending the infant to God, and they set a headstone made of wood in place. It had been hurriedly made, with Nia's name carved roughly into the wood.

Anne stayed a long time at the grave site after the others had left. She watched the rose underbelly of the sunset glow like the belly of a dragon. The clouds overhead faded, greying away, and softening into their great blue-grey milieu while the horizon burned gold, then fiery orange, finally simmering down into greyness as well.

* * *

Peter's shoe scraped on the floor of the safe room as he shifted his position uncomfortably. This crouching and sitting was hard for him and for Bess, Anne knew. Bess was unaccountably quiet, and Anne wondered if she was thinking of the damage to the house. She felt her own damp nervousness upon her brow and the metal shelving behind her dug into her back. She stood up and stretched. The light from the window was growing dimmer as the evening came on. As she sat again, Devon stood and began pacing. His form broke through the glimmer from the window and chopped it up into light and dark bands as his tall legs moved back and forth. His footsteps seemed loud on the concrete floor, though it was only because everyone's senses were heightened. Nasiche finally gestured angrily at him to sit down and he did so with a grunt of frustration. The waiting seemed interminable. There was still the sound of faint voices in the house, though no more loud crashes. Joy fiddled with her long-braided hair, twisting it in her fingers. She and Mila whispered together with worried expressions. Anne wondered if they would all end up being killed, and on the news, back in the States. What would her mother feel?

Two weeks before the trip to Uganda, Anne reluctantly told her mother of her plans. Her mother's face had been pale. "You'll be gone for two whole years? Do you really think you can do that?" her mother had asked. "I mean, you'll be terribly homesick. You know how you were in college when you went away to that camp in the summer."

Anne felt a surge of anger that her mother would bring up the failure. That was eight years ago, and she was a different person now. Couldn't her mother understand that she had her own life to live? She wasn't a child anymore. Anne saw the sudden tears come to her mother's eyes, and the old guilt pulled at her. Her mother was a kind woman, and would miss her. She couldn't understand how damaged Anne had been from her huand's alcoholism. Somehow Anne knew that if she made a more permanent break, she could be the person she was meant to be. "Don't just disappear," begged her mother. "Write or call every week. Anne nodded and hugged her, realizing that she probably wouldn't follow through. Contact with her mother felt like a chain holding her to a dismal past. Her mother didn't understand because she had kept in contact with her own mother 'Nana' twice a week for as long as Anne could remember – more often as the older woman had grown feebler. Yet, the strange thing was that Anne knew her mother felt coerced into it as well. Her mother had once confided to Anne that when she had her "face done," which was her face lift, Anne's mother knew the procedure would be unacceptable to Nana. Indulgent. She had stayed away in person only by pretending to be ill. When she finally visited Nana three weeks later, Nana did not guess, only saying that her daughter looked 'rested.'

In the safe room, Anne smiled thinking of this rare moment – her mother sharing a confidence with her. It was a secret Anne had never told. She considered. Reluctantly, the question arose again. Had God truly called her to Uganda? Or had her desire to get away from home caused her to imagine it? She certainly didn't feel equipped to deal with the poverty and hardship she had encountered here. Everything had gone wrong. And if she had simply thought she heard God's voice, but really hadn't…? Somehow, that would confirm her worst fears – that God wasn't really guiding her. And if that were true, maybe she wasn't really His child after all.

There was a flash of brightness through the window, bringing Anne back to the present. Carefully she made her way over and could see through the window grate and the branches of a bush the light of torches over by the school. She stumbled over Peter's legs and made her way to Bess. "Torches" she whispered to Bess, and Bess nodded.

Bess was well aware of the danger and had built the safe room for this very reason. Terrorism in Uganda had occurred primarily in the north and West, often connected to the Islamic State. A school on the western border of Uganda had recently been attacked and forces from the Democratic Republic of Congo blamed for the massacre. It was always a possibility even in Kampala.

Bess felt the dryness of her own lips and wished they had stocked the room with water. She also wished for a flashlight – one more thing she now thought of too late. But then again, the light might have alerted the marauders to their hiding place. The occasional flicker from the torches caused eerie shadows to play across the room. The arthritis in her back was also causing her some pain. She changed her position slightly, leaning back onto a bag of rice. It gave her more support. She was not afraid for her own safety so much as for those in her charge. She looked over at the others, especially at Joy and Mila. The responsibility was a heavy weight.

***

The van was in working order again. Bess arrived home from the eight- hour trip with three of the seminary students. She felt tired and grouchy, but brightened when she entered the kitchen, as she always did when she saw her adopted daughters. As they sat at the table for dinner, she recalled for them the difficult day, and let herself express her irritation. They had been to visit a pastor in a village outside of Masindi, to deliver some money and give encouragement, but on the way back they had been stopped by the authorities. The Ugandan police were corrupt and always looking to be paid a bribe. They claimed that the luggage rack on the top of the van was not regulation because it had not been cleared. Bess had used her most servile voice to address the police man. She knew from experience that anything less met with more resistance. "Sir," Bess had pleaded. "It has been this way for ten years. Your own people waved the need for clearance at that time. We have been driving it for ten years. Please call someone and you will find out." He was unrelenting. "Sir," she said. "*Please* call someone. *Please. Please* don't take away our van."

Bess straightened her silverware. "He wanted money, but we have no more money to give them. He wanted me to offer him a bribe."

"What happened?" asked Joy.

"Thank God for Dembe." Said Bess. "It turns out the official was from Mbale. Dembe is also from Mbale and spoke Lugisu with him, and talked him into letting us go. They knew some of the same people."

Elaine's eyes opened wide. "Answer to prayer, surely."

"I was praying," affirmed Noah.

Elaine nodded encouragingly to him.

"Thank goodness for Noah as well," said Bess. She sighed and looked at the group at the table. "The government has never liked the compound. They've done all they could do to shove us out. And we've fought with our church in the States as well. They never approved of a woman being in charge. We 've been fighting since Robert passed away, and only lately have begun making progress. Thank goodness for Pastor John Smith. He's fought for us." Bess was aware that Joy and Mila knew this background, but Anne was new.

She worried about Anne. The young woman was so talented, so idealistic, and so headstrong at times. In some ways Bess saw a younger version of herself in Anne. Bess recalled the hopes and dreams she and Robert had come to Uganda with. It had been difficult, but they had leaned on each other when finances were tight, or barriers were erected against them. They had found the need to teach the students not only bible, but moral principles as well – honesty, hard work, even punctuality had been lacking. Christianity in Uganda was a mile wide but an inch thick. Full of emotion and the belief that God would provide not just blessings, but riches. Foreigners too, that came to Uganda, felt badly for the Ugandans and gave money, but they didn't understand that such a thing was not necessarily helpful. Robert had been the primary impetus in the Ugandan's education. Then when Robert died, along with his energy, she thought she would never make it on her own. Then Elaine had come, and look what God had done. She looked around the table proudly, appreciating each face, her gaze traveling from one to the next. As her eyes fell on Anne, her worry was recalled. Bess sensed that Anne was depressed over something. Did she miss the States? Or did it have to do with the mission compound and what she was asked to do? Bess was aware that Anne had initially placed her on a pedestal, and that now perhaps that pedestal was collapsing. If so, Anne would have to deal with the emotional aftermath.

Bess's reverie was broken as voices and then shouting came from what sounded like outside the high compound walls. Then there were loud ringing sounds, as though metal were being beaten on metal. Everyone paused. Devon jumped up and went out the door to look. In a few moments he flew back, gesticulating toward the side of the compound.

"Someone is coming," he said, the white of his eyes showing wider. "Someone is breaking down the gate."

"How can they break down the gate?" asked Bess firmly.

"I believe they are pounding off the hinges," said Devon.

The meal was suspended abruptly.

"Quickly," said Bess, and now she was all action, though her stomach dropped. "Everyone into the safe room!"

Everyone scrambled, and only Mila remembered to shoo Sampson out from beneath the table and cajole him down the steps.

* * *

Nasiche held Gabriel on her lap. She had shushed him for so long, he had finally fallen asleep. She shifted her stiff legs. There had been some whispering, and everyone agreed it was not the police – it was a Muslim faction that had broken in. It was in retaliation for the help they had given Ayesha and her baby. Now they were destroying and looting. Nasiche was afraid they would set the house on fire. She clutched Gabriel closer.

Anne watched at the window again as the torches bobbed in and out of her sight. Peter coughed. Everyone's nerves were stretched. After all the waiting and silence, though, Anne's thoughts were becoming more focused. She knew there was a good chance Ayesha had been killed because she had left the Muslim faith. Everyone here believed it was so.

The big house had contributed to Ayesha's conversion, and the brother knew she had come for bible study. They must have staked out the complex weeks ago. Was that what they wanted – to destroy the compound? Or was there more? A thought hovered in her subconscious, just out of reach. She exhaled, frustrated. As she relaxed, she became aware of the rhythm of her own breath and the smothering sensation of the room. Then, the thought came to her. They were looking for the baby. They didn't know the baby was dead. That's why they were searching through every room, and were now searching the school as well. Perhaps Ayesha's father was out there right now, looking for his grandchild. When they didn't find the infant, maybe they would indeed burn the house down.

Now, in the growing darkness, the faces of Anne's companions were less distinguishable. She could make out the white of Bess's arms and face, and the bright colors of Elaine's dress. The dark skin of the Ugandans melted into the shadow. An idea began to take shape in Anne's mind, and she pushed gently on the grate covering the window. To her surprise it flipped upward, hinged only at the top. She moved back into the room, the discovery slightly unnerving her, but also giving her fresh courage. What if, she wondered, the idea forming more clearly, the baby's body was given to the Muslims – to the grandfather. What if someone could bring it to him? Perhaps they would leave. Anne's heart pounded at the thought. She considered the two men in the room, as well as Bess and Elaine. They were too big to get through the small window. Nasiche had Gabriel, and Kissa was able, but would Kissa? No. Before it had gotten so dark, Anne had seen her huddled on the floor, terrified. Anne was slender. She could perhaps get through the window. She began formulating the plan. Desperate, yes, but possible. However, she had to move quickly before anyone stopped her. She stepped silently again over Peter's legs and made her way back to the window. She knew she was being reckless, and possibly could be killed, but now she felt positively giddy with adrenaline. Before anyone could react, she had levered herself onto the windowsill, worked her shoulders through the opening and slithered through the window.

The night was black, but the moon was just rising. Anne stumbled around the bush and then almost tripped over an edging of brick surrounding a flower garden. Over to her left she heard voices, and saw the flash of the torches. Keeping to her right, she skirted the lawn to stay in the shadows until finally making her way to the south side. Blundering painfully into a rose bush, she extricated herself carefully from the thorns. She ignored her stinging flesh and crawled through carefully to the burial site. She reached in to where she knew the soft dirt of the grave would be easy to dig up with her hands. Instead of the mound of dirt, she encountered a hole. She searched frantically, digging with her fingers, a piece of hair swinging in her face, her face now dirty as she attempted to push her hair away. The small body was gone! At that moment Anne heard a noise behind her. She rose and swung around. In the light of the just rising moon, she saw the brown-skinned man with the pock-marked face. He was the very man they had seen on the street during their search for Ayesha's address. Though it had been several months, she recognized him. In his arms he held a dirty white bundle – the small remains of Nia.

Anne was shocked, but the man did not threaten her. She moved from the rosebushes and stood, ready to flee at any moment. "I have come for to help you" he said in broken English.

"Oh," said Anne, at a loss.

"Trouble, it has been brewing," the man continued. "With my friends. I know they were planning to come here. You remember me?"

Ann nodded.

"I am called Aabid. I heard what you say on the street at the mosque," he continued.

"And you want to help?" asked Anne.

He was a Muslim like all the rest, dressed in the traditional robe, as he had been dressed previously in the street.

"I know Ayesha's father" said the pock-marked man.

He handed the bundle to her and Anne felt the lightness of the skeletal remains. Aabid took Anne's shoulder, leading her toward the torches.

"I was going to bring to him the baby. But perhaps it is better for you to do."

Ann had the feeling she was being led to a firing squad. As they approached the affronted clan, some of them stopped and looked. Then, as though in agreement, several of them made a rush towards her. Aabid stepped in front of Anne, warding them off with his hands. He spoke rapidly and loudly in a tongue unknown to Anne, and she saw them pause. Aabid waved them away. When an older man in a turban stepped forward, the conversation continued. Anne could see an excited anger in the older man and he pounded his fist into his hand. Then Aabid gently guided

Anne towards him, and trembling, Anne placed the bundle in the older man's arms.

"He wants to know from you what happened," said Aabid.

Then Anne explained everything. She told how Nia had grown sick with malaria. How she had been taken to the hospital and given medication, but that the medication had not worked. Aabid translated. Then Anne spoke of how the baby had been buried within twenty-four hours. How she had been washed and wrapped. Aabid agreed, nodding, adding in English that the infant's head had been pointed toward Mecca. This he also translated to the old man.

Finally, the old man's head drooped. He opened the white cloth and looked on the small skeleton. Then abruptly he turned and walked away with it. The others followed, and Anne and Aabid watched them go. Just before exiting over the broken gate, one of the men tossed his torch in a moment of defiance. It arched and landed on top of a small shed near the church. It began to smolder, but Anne and Aabid stood motionless until the men disappeared into the night. Then they rushed to pour water and stamp out the rising flames.

CHAPTER EIGHT

BESS EMERGED FROM THE SAFE ROOM AND HOUSE WITH others following her. Even after an explanation, her anger flared at Anne.

"What business was it of yours to not say a word – to leave us- we who are responsible for your safety and take a risk like that? You could have easily been killed!"

The feeling of impotence Bess had had in the safe room – increased by the moment she discovered that Anne was gone - made her momentarily irate. Anne took it all, standing in a posture of servitude before her. Aabid stood unnoticed off to the side. Finally, when Bess had exhausted her fury, her demeaner changed. She hugged Anne firmly and lastly acknowledged Aabid. When the details of his part in the drama emerged, she thanked him.

"How is it that you ended up coming here?" Bess asked Aabid.

"When I heard your people looking for Ayesha on the streets, I follow them and listen to them speak together of the baby. I knew my people would come here," he explained. "I joined, but went to look for a grave."

"We are most grateful for your help in the situation," said Bess.

"I do not believe in retribution, despite what Allah might say," replied Aabid gravely. "Allah also invites us to the Home of Peace and guides whom He will to a straight path."

"Well, thank God, He guided you here. Will you stay for coffee and talk longer?" she asked. She was curious to know more of Aabid, but Aabid declined.

After Aabid was gone, Bess surveyed the damage. In the kitchen, dishes had been smashed, and several chairs broken. The bedding in the bedrooms had been pulled off the beds, and some of the drawers of the dressers removed, their contents dumped on the floor. One of the bookshelves in Bess's study had been knocked over, the books scattered. There was no major damage except for the gate, half of which lay on the ground, the hinges twisted. Bess sighed. Repairs would have to wait until morning.

"Everyone, get to bed," she commanded. "Tomorrow is soon enough to set things right."

The next day the women straightened up at the house. Only minimal damage was found at the school, where a door had been battered in. Nasiche and Kissa reported their quarters had also been entered, and Gabriel's clothing and playthings gone through. The male students, guided by Bess and Elaine worked to repair the chairs and put a new roof on the shed. Joseph went to town to find a new door for the school.

"They are hard workers," remarked Anne, observing the students.

"We try and teach them Christian ethics and responsibility," replied Elaine. "Most of the time they do well."

It ended up taking more time than expected to fix the gate and replace the hinges, so there was a feeling of insecurity in the compound until that was accomplished. Afterwards, there was an inward sigh of relief, but also the awareness that if the gates had been breached once, it could be done again.

Anne met with Bess in her office. The large desk was piled as usual with papers. The bookshelves and books were all back in their places.

"I apologize again," said Anne. "I should have discussed my thoughts in the safe room with you – about the baby."

"Yes, you should have," said Bess.

"I was just afraid you wouldn't agree to the plan, I guess."

Bess smiled slightly. "I probably wouldn't have," she admitted. "And God intervened. But you must see there is authority that must be followed. We also work as a team."

Anne nodded.

"There are no lone rangers here," went on Bess. "No one person out on their own."

This made Anne think of the reason she had come.

"That's why I came," confessed Anne. "The last time I was here..." she paused, trying to formulate the words. "It was like, - like heaven, with everybody loving each other...."
She stopped, embarrassed, but Bess looked at her kindly.

"Sometimes I used to feel like that too," Bess said. "Like heaven. I think it's the touch of God's Spirit. I'm glad you've reminded me of it."

"But everything has fallen apart," said Anne. "I'm feeling so confused and thinking maybe I should go back to the States."

Bess was silent. "Pray about it," she finally said. "Think and pray about it before you decide. We'll talk again."

The next few mornings dawned bright but there was a slight coolness in the air that heralded the coming of autumn. Bess discussed the need to take some supplies given them to the orphanage in Hoima. She also knew that Bitalo had not visited his village for many months, so she suggested he go along and they stop there on the way. Elaine, Anne, and Joseph would join Bitalo, with Devon driving of course. They would all go to the village and then deliver supplies to the orphanage. Bitalo's village was about five hours away, and Hoima was not far from there.

"Have you ever been to the game preserve before?" Bess asked Anne in front of the others, as though it were a last-minute thought.

"No ma'am," Anne acknowledged.

"You must all go after you visit the orphanage. It is a wonderful place." Bess assured her. "You can't visit Uganda without seeing the animals. All of you can spend the night before you come back."

Anne wondered why this graciousness was being extended to her. Was it because of the harrowing break-in, or because of her thoughts of cutting her time in Uganda short?

In the van, Anne sat next to Elaine. Anne had always felt a sense of intimidation around the other woman, but now she found Elaine quite personable. Elaine confided that she was dealing with a situation – or trying to deal with it. It had to do with one of the church members. He was so angry at her, and she was trying to meet him in a calm manner and listen and respond. However, he would get so upset he would shout at her. This had gone on over and over.

"The culture is so different here," she confided to Anne. "I'm still trying to find my way."

"Perhaps they see women differently than in the States."

"That's definitely part of it," agreed Elaine.

Anne also learned that Elaine had contracted Malaria within months of arriving in Uganda.

"It was ghastly," said Elaine. "I was flown back to the States, but they really don't know how to treat malaria there. I practically died. Most everyone here has had malaria at least once, and then it can be recurrent."

As they passed through Kampala, the noise and bustle grew. One truck packed with longhorn steers passed on the side. The sidewalks were jammed as usual with colorful fruit stalls, and Anne saw beautifully carved wooden furniture for sale sitting outside in the dirt. Headboards for bedroom sets were numerous. Anne hoped it wouldn't rain because the clouds were building. What would the sellers do with the furniture if it rained? She supposed they would cover it, rather than trying to haul it inside. A little further along she saw mannequins dressed in tight-fitting women's clothing. They were arrayed in short skirts, high heels, and stylishly cut jackets.

"It looks like those fashions could have come from the U.S," Anne mentioned to Elaine, surprised.

"Some of the young people in the city are wanting to imitate the United States," said Elaine. "Traditional long skirts though are still the norm for most, especially in the more rural areas."

Anne nodded. She had been warned against wearing shorts or short skirts anywhere but on the compound. She had been told that the older the woman, the longer the skirt. Accordingly, she was allowed calf-length skirts, while Bess wore her to her ankles. Elaine seemed to like giving out information so Anne took advantage of it.

"The buildings – some of them look quite ornate,"

mentioned Anne. "But at the same time so much of it looks run down."

"You're right," replied Elaine. "The big structures in stone were built by the British. They colonized the area in the 1800's. Uganda was granted its independence in 1962. But everything has gotten old, and the Ugandans haven't repaired the buildings."

"They don't seem very professional," said Anne.

"No. Professionalism is not really a word for Uganda. No one has taught them. Things are changing, but it happens slowly," said Elaine.

As they continued, the larger buildings were replaced by poorer looking ones. Soon they were out of the city and into the countryside. Anne looked out at the wide-open landscape. She saw Mountains and asked Elaine about them.

"There are twenty-one mountain peaks around Kampala," said Elaine. "Unfortunately, the forested areas are being replaced by more desert-like conditions. That's why you see all the Elephant grass. They cut down all the trees in the north, and the desert is spreading." She sighed. "They don't know that trees hold the soil, too, so mudslides wipe out countless villages."

They lapsed into silence and Anne enjoyed the view for the next several hours. As they drove Anne felt the temperature rising. Elaine pointed out the Rwenzori Mountains in the distance to the west.

"Those mountains," Elaine instructed, "have Africa's third highest peak, and are the only permanently snow-capped mountains on the equator."

"Beautiful" said Anne.

After another hour, Anne began seeing small round huts

with pointed roofs. Some of them were arranged in groups of four or five. Many seemed to have no windows. Individuals along the road stopped to look as the van went by.

"What are those little huts?" asked Anne.

"Village homes," said Elaine. "Made of mud and sticks, and the roofs are thatched. The people here are very poor. Bitalo's village is similar."

"How soon until we get there?" Anne yawned. She was feeling tired from the ride, and longed to get out and stretch her legs.

"Not long now."

Indeed, shortly after they arrived at the village. The van was greeted by a string of women dancing along beside it until they had parked. Enthusiasm ran high and shrill ululation and clapping met Anne and Elaine as they stepped off the van. It was as if they were engulfed in a greeting of high-pitched celebratory trills. Some of the women had on colorful dresses with puffed sleeves, a square neck, and a sash below the waist and over the hips. Children surrounded everywhere.

"Word must have gotten out that we were coming," said Elaine, smiling. They are wearing their very finest."

Just like a party, thought Anne, as she and Elaine raised their arms and danced along with the others.

Chairs had been set out for them under a tree, and the visitors were served sodas, apparently purchased for the occasion. Anne knew the water was bad, but the colas were ok. Children surrounded the group and stared at them wide-eyed. Elaine explained that some of the younger ones had probably never seen anyone with white skin. One little boy came up to Anne and touched her hair. Anne smiled at him and held out her arms to hold him, but he shyly withdrew. There was no way to communicate but by smiles, and gestures, and Elaine whispered that they spoke Nyoro. Bitalo was able to translate, but could only be in one conversation at a time. Then they found that the village chief also spoke English. Elaine was interested in asking questions of him, and Bitalo introduced Anne to some of his family members, taking her and Joseph aside to another grassy area. Here, Bitalo explained, is where they would pray.

"Pray?" asked Anne.

"Yes," replied Bitalo seriously. "There are many here who are sick and in need of prayer. They are asking if you would pray for them."

One villager after another knelt before Anne while she prayed for them.

"Put your hand on their heads" instructed Bitalo.

With each one, Bitalo would listen attentively and then tell Anne the difficulty, and she would pray. "This one has pain in the stomach," Bitalo would say. Or "this one is blind in the right eye." Or, "this one is having bad dreams."

Anne could see no discernable difference from her prayers, but the villagers seemed to have faith enough. One young woman who seemed quite agitated was brought by another, older man.

He spoke to Bitalo, who reported to Anne – "This one is affected by a demon. Her father says she has tried to kill herself many times. He would like you to pray that the demon would be cast away."

"What is her name?" asked Anne.

She felt quite out of her depth in praying for the woman, whose name she found was Bertha, and was glad when

Bitalo motioned Joseph over to pray as well. As Anne prayed, she felt the warmth of the woman's head, but no other perceptible change. Afterwards, many people reached out their hands towards Anne, and she grasped them. One woman reached out her hand but seemed to impatiently wave away Anne's touch.

Bitalo led Anne away, saying "that one wants money." Before leaving the village, Bitalo wanted Anne to meet someone. "He is very old," said Bitalo. "He is considered unusual because of his white hair."

Bitalo led Anne to the small hut down the road and then entered with permission and sat while the old man welcomed them. The interior was cool. He and Bitalo spoke while Anne smiled.

Then the old man addressed her and Bitalo translated. "He says he is glad you were called to come to Uganda."

The old man's face was wrinkled, his mouth toothless. His white hair was like cotton, but the eyes under their straggly brows were clear. He seemed to Anne to know more about her than Bitalo had revealed.

For some reason she felt compelled to confess "I don't know that I was called at all to come here. Perhaps it was a horrible mistake."

This was translated by Bitalo before she could take it back. The old man spoke, smiling and nodding, and Anne thought perhaps he hadn't gotten the message.

But Bitalo translated back "If you believe you are called then you are. It is not easy to come to Uganda."

As Anne and the others got back on the van the villagers waved goodbye.

After they had exited the area, Elaine came to Joseph

and Anne, and said, "I heard about Bertha. I am going to pray for you both because when you pray regarding demonic activity, there can be an attack."

She then prayed, and Anne thanked her afterward, saying "but I don't know that any demon was actually cast from the poor woman."

Elaine shrugged. "Her father is positive it was. He said the oppression has left her."

As they drove on, Anne's thoughts buzzed with the experiences at the village, and the trip to the orphanage seemed very short. There again the children greeted them, wanting to hold Anne's purse and phone for her. Anne allowed one little girl with a stick-like frame and a wide smile almost too big for her face to hold her phone, while Bitalo and Joseph unloaded boxes of various items for the orphanage. In the boxes were crayons and paper, diapers, soccer balls, and backpacks for the children. Everyone was thrilled and the little boys took off across the uneven grass with one of the balls, yelling wildly.

A small group of orphanage "mothers" were gathered at the edge of the orphanage property watching at a group of men with shovels working fifty yards away. Elaine went over to talk with the women, while Anne sat on a concrete step and played with one of the toddlers. His tiny plump hands pulled at her beaded necklace as he sat on her lap. She noticed that all the children were dressed alike in uniforms, the boys in shorts and the girls in dresses. All had their heads shaved. She decided it was to keep away the lice.

When Elaine came back, she pointed back to the group still gathered, intent on watching the men.

"There are men over there, filling in a well," she said. "It was dug, but it was right next to a latrine so they're filling it back in."

Anne picked up the toddler, disengaging him from her necklace, and set him aside, while she stood.

"It's time we got going," said Elaine.

The visit had been short, and Anne was impressed when the little girl who had her phone respectfully gave it back. Elaine laughed and said – "check your pictures. You may have some extra ones on there." Anne smiled, feeling a sudden sense of well-being. It had been a good day – and now she was looking forward to seeing the animals.

CHAPTER NINE

THE ANIMAL PRESERVE WAS MADE UP OF MILES OF protected land. Before setting out on their safari, everyone went to their rooms and rested. Anne had a private room with a queen size bed, a flushable toilet, and a shower with an actual curtain around it. She felt she was basking in luxury. After examining the room, she wandered into the resort lobby. The others were occupied elsewhere, so she sat on one of the rich leather chairs and picked up a glossy magazine printed in color. It was written in English for its guests and Anne thumbed through it looking at pictures of wildlife. She read an article that described Uganda. It had been quoted by Churchill as being the "pearl of Africa," because of its diversity and beauty.

Anne stepped outside. Here was a beautifully manicured lawn and a pool off to the side. Chairs were scattered about for casual seating, and further away, a swing. On the other side of the lawn, so close you could practically swim in it - was lake Albert. Anne wandered outside, and looked curiously at a small orange and blue gecko on a nearby tree. At the swing she sat, gazing at the large expanse of water before her. Then she leaned over and lay down, the wooden seat twisting slightly with her weight. She looked upward. The sky was pale at the horizon line but deepened overhead to a rich blue the color of cobalt. Her thought was that the sky here looked just like the sky she had left in New Mexico.

The same enormous blossom of white clouds beginning to build. The same sky half a world apart.

She could hear Joseph and Bitalo, over at the pool, splashing about, and playing some kind of game. She brought her knees up, the back of the swing hiding her from sight. Soon she fell asleep.

Anne was awakened by someone shouting her name. Lifting her head she saw Joseph, on the lawn.

"We've been searching for you," said Joseph, looking relieved. "The jeep is about to leave for the safari."

"Oh my," said Anne, looking at her watch. "I can't believe I slept so long."

It was now late afternoon, a little after five o'clock. She jumped up and hurriedly followed Joseph to the waiting vehicle. The others were already seated. There were three rows of seats, the first being for the driver and someone beside him. The next row of three seats were up higher, and the last row of two seats were higher still; several steps up and just below the top canopy. Anne made her way just behind and above the driver and sat beside Joseph.

The jeep turned down the dirt road onto a paved section and sped on. Soon they turned off again onto dirt. The jeep went more slowly now, everyone looking out at the surrounding countryside. Umbrella-like trees displayed their wide canopies, and the tall knee-high grass and savanna stretched in every direction. The animals were plentiful. On the right, Joseph pointed out baby wart hogs. *They are so cute,* thought Anna, for when they ran, they each followed the other in a line, their little tails stuck straight up in the air. They were quick, and would race off before she could get her camera in place. Dozens of antelopes dotted the landscape, and she could see them leaping gracefully. When the jeep stopped to let some giraffes cross the road, Anne thought with amused exhilaration, how it was like cattle crossing in the States. The giraffes swayed forward and back, and stepped in a funny swinging motion. The driver pointed out the little horns on their heads. The males had thicker horns, he said, and were larger. The older the giraffe, the darker its spots.

"Look at that old one," Joseph said, as a tall giraffe walked gracefully by.

After the giraffes had crossed, the jeep continued, and it became obvious that the driver was looking for lions. Then he stopped the jeep, and in the distance, they could see a small form on top of a rocky outcrop that was apparently a lion. Everyone became excited and the driver took a detour off the road and through the grass, hoping to circle behind. Finally, after wild driving and swerving around rocks, the jeep pulled up and ahead they could all see a lioness, lying in the sun.

"Do not get any closer," warned the driver, for they had all disembarked and gotten out their cell phones. As they watched and snapped pictures, the lioness rose and walked along a log, posing perfectly for a moment before disappearing in the grass.

The safari was already a success, as it was not every time that you saw a lion. Anne was also intrigued at the many varieties of antelope. There were little tiny ones that the driver identified as the Dik Dik. Then there was a tall one with a long snout and elegant ribbed horns. It was so funny looking with its elongated face, and Anne asked the driver what it was. He replied that it was a Hartebeest. It was one of the fastest creatures, he said, and could easily outrun a lion. However, added the driver, it also had a small brain. After running for a while, it would forget why it was running, and stop. Then the lion would catch it.

Here and there were mud puddles, with African buffalo wallowing in, or standing around near the mud. They had square noses, and it looked to Anne that they had horns that seemed to be parted directly in the middle as someone might part their hair. The horns then curved down and out on either side. *They look like they're wearing wigs,* she thought to herself. Perched on the buffalo's backs were tiny yellow and red beaked birds, that Anne learned were called oxpeckers. They ate the tics and lice off the larger animals.

Next, everyone was engaged for a time in looking for leopards in the trees. The driver said they liked to lay out on the branches, sometimes with their legs dangling down. None were seen, and they finally pulled in to a marshy area near the lake. Anne walked out with the others to the water to get a good view and eat a granola bar provided. Each person wandered off separately for a while, enjoying the solitude, before reboarding the jeep. Anne felt a great sense of gratitude. What a memorable experience. It was just as one would picture Africa from the movies. On the way back, Anne saw a herd of elephants in the distance. She breathed a silent prayer that she might see them up closer, but the jeep turned away down another path. On the way back there were more giraffe, buffalo, and antelope, and the driver pointed out what might have been a hyena, but it was distant. Arriving back at the lodge just after a beautiful sunset, they were invited to a late dinner out on the porch.

That evening, instead of going to bed, Anne went

back outside and sat out on one of the chairs on the grass. Her imagination was fired from the day of activity, but she felt calm and happy. The evening air wafted over her, and there was a touch of lilac in the smell of it. She let her body relax, and her limbs felt weightless. Closing her eyes, she spoke to God then, telling Him her doubts and her disappointments. She had imagined a ministry where she would always feel Him directing her, working through her, accomplishing her goals, like some type of unseen hand in her life. Instead, she had felt frustration and challenges in every direction. She thought of Ayesha and Nia, and Fatuma and Adroa – and saw her failure. Surely the others – Bess and Elaine- were guided with more assurance. But then she realized simultaneously that this was not always true. Bess had struggles with the authorities, with the church. Elaine had shared her difficulties with a church member. Even so, they were called to the ministry.

Anne looked out into the growing darkness. If things were only easier. But then love was not always easy. It really shouldn't be. Because of Anne's alcoholic father, her mother had always stepped in to try and make things smooth – doing all she could for Anne – but that had not really helped Anne. Her mother's 'help' had kept her from learning to do things herself, feeling confidence, developing the perseverance needed. She considered. But she wanted a concrete answer. Was she called? She had always desired to be a missionary. Was that enough? What had the old man in the village said? Something about the fact that if she had gotten here, she was called? Of course, God did not speak audibly from heaven. Maybe He wasn't that exacting either. That was a pleasant thought, and she let her mind dwell on it. Could it be that

He was happy with her attempts, flawed as they were? She recalled her bible study ladies and the joy they brought her. She thought of the demon-oppressed Bertha that God had delivered with very little help from Anne. She was part of something bigger than herself - and she had been willing. Perhaps that was the only real key.

In the gloaming, the crescent moon shone and made the nearby water cast its reflection back in a thousand tiny slivers. The grass was black and wet; the shadows deep. Anne heard a rustling sound and then a movement, and the air was displaced by a giant weight. The form of an elephant emerged from beneath the trees, followed by a second, smaller one. They walked along the lawn, their large ears flapping lightly, the baby elephant grasping its mother's tail with its trunk, the mother's trunk swinging gently. They were unaware of any intruder, and Anne sat frozen, watching the giant beasts in awe.

When they had passed, Anne continued to sit. A sense of royalty enveloped her. She felt God's gracious answer to her earlier prayer, and to all her prayers. She felt His personal embrace.

The next morning Anne awoke early despite the late night. She opened her eyes. The sun was shining, filtering through the thin curtains, penetrating the mosquito netting. She sat up. She remembered the night before. It was like awakening and recalling the wonderful dream one had just had. She also had a distinct feeling - a knowing that came from outside herself. She suddenly knew she was called to Uganda - not to give of her paltry self, but to receive, and only out of that to give back. The ego itself had no place. She sighed contentedly. Sitting with her notepad, she recorded her thoughts and emotions in the form of a poem. Just recently she had found that poetry was a powerful outlet. Satisfied, she put her pen down. It was almost time to meet with the others for breakfast, and then the trip back - and soon, she decided, she would write to her mother.

A POEM

The women carry Uganda on their backs
and all other things
on their heads.
What poise as they carry their loads
of poverty and sorrow.
The village dances with fury
accompanying our bus to its stop,
and the children greet us with screams
of joy and kneel before us
as though we were royalty.
Such beautiful smiles on each face.
I am too full to tell you
of my grief and shame
For I am rich and own too much
and I am poor and love too little.
Uganda is a place of beauty and sorrow
dignified yet corrupt
and I want to flee home
and shake off its awful heat
and biting tsetse flies and risk of malaria
and the mosquito nets that don't cover the beds,
and the spotty electricity and broken technology
in the finest hotels.
The missionaries shrug and say "This is Uganda"
and it will linger in my unconsciousness and dreams
whether I will it or not.